Wyland's Spouty and Friends

An Underwater Journey Through the A, B, Seas

Created by Marine Life Artist Wyland for children everywhere

Written by Steve Creech and Designed by Gregg Hamby

Wyland Worldwide, LLC
5 Columbia
Aliso Viejo, CA 92656
Phone 949-643-7070
Fax 949-643-7099
www.wyland.com
wylandpublishing@wyland.com

Printed and bound in the United States

Produced by:
Wyland Worldwide, LLC
5 Columbia
Aliso Viejo, CA 92656

1 3 5 7 9 10 8 6 4 2

Library of Congress Cataloging-in-Publication Data

Wyland, 1956
Spouty and Friends
An Underwater Journey Through the A,B, Seas
Text by Wyland/Steve Creech

ISBN 1-884840-59-0

Special thanks to Wyland Design, Gregg Hamby, Steve Creech,
Gino Beltran, Tina Wu, Karla Kipp and Kathy Gordon.

Creative Production: Wyland Design
Printing: Precision Offset
Marketing and Distribution: Angela Needham

**Wyland's
Spouty and Friends:
An Underwater Journey Through the A, B, Seas**

make an impression

Wyland Books
The Art of Wyland © 1992
Whale Tales © 1995
Wyland: The Whaling Walls © 1997
The Undersea World of Wyland © 1998
Wyland: Ocean Wisdom © 2000
Wyland: Artist of the Sea © 2002
Chicken Soup for the Ocean Lover's Soul © 2003
Wyland's Spouty and Friends: An Underwater Journey
Through the A, B, Seas © 2004
America's Artists: The Artists of Wyland Galleries © 2004

This book is dedicated to all the children

whose curiosity and love for nature

remind us every day

about the wonders of our world.

WYLAND

Down we go ...

Where boats cannot sail ...

To visit the home
of Spouty the whale . . .

From A to Z let's see where he goes.

Let's meet all the creatures and friends that he knows.

A is for Angel,
swimming along.

B

B is for Blue whales,

singing a song.

C is for Crusty,
a turtle most rare.

D

D is for Delphi,
who hasn't a care.

E

E is for Everything,
like fish or a whale.

F is the Flick of a
thresher shark's tail.

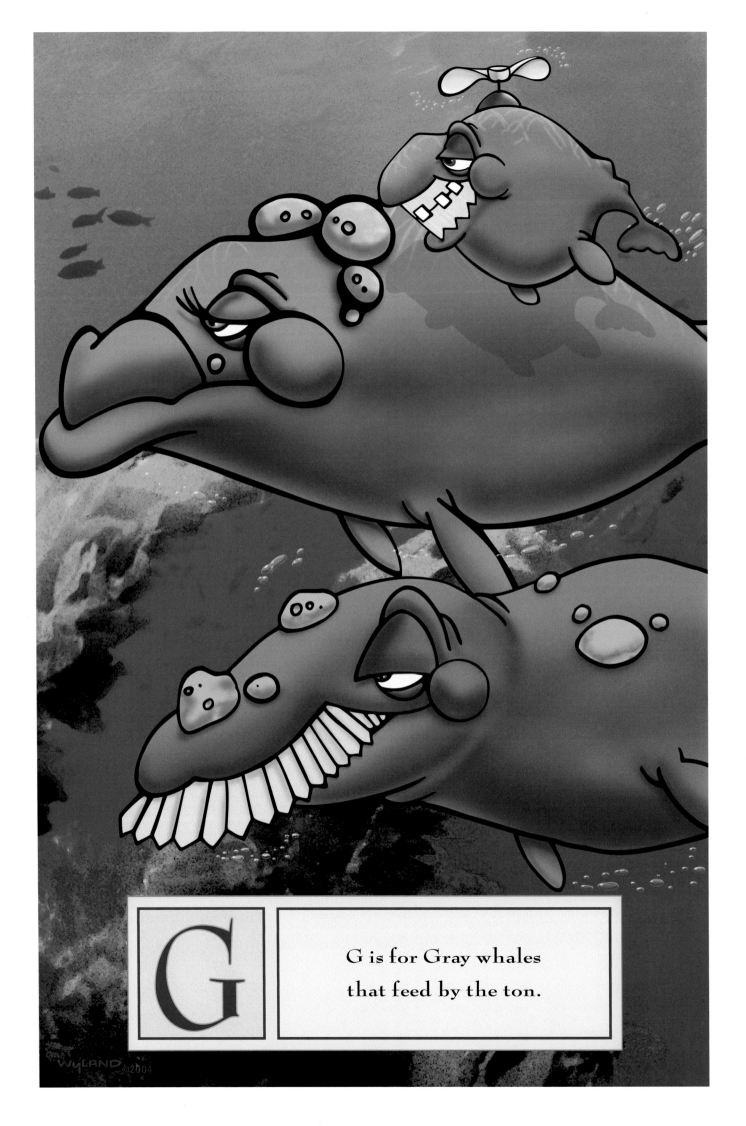

G

G is for Gray whales
that feed by the ton.

H is for "Hugh" manatee,
who loves to have fun.

I is for the Indigo
of octopus ink.

J

J is for Jellyfish,
colored red, blue and pink.

K

K is for Killer,
the "KING" of the sea.

L

L is for "Lu" seal,
so playful and free.

M

M is for Manta,
a curious sight.

N

N is a Nautilus
that floats up at night.

O

O is for Otter,
who zips through the sea.

P

P is for Princess,
a sea horse is she.

Q

Q is for Quiet creatures
that dwell in the deep.

R

R is for Right whales
that float when they sleep.

S is for Sammy,
a shark with a bite.

T is a Triggerfish,
darting from sight.

U

U is Unusual,

as some creatures are.

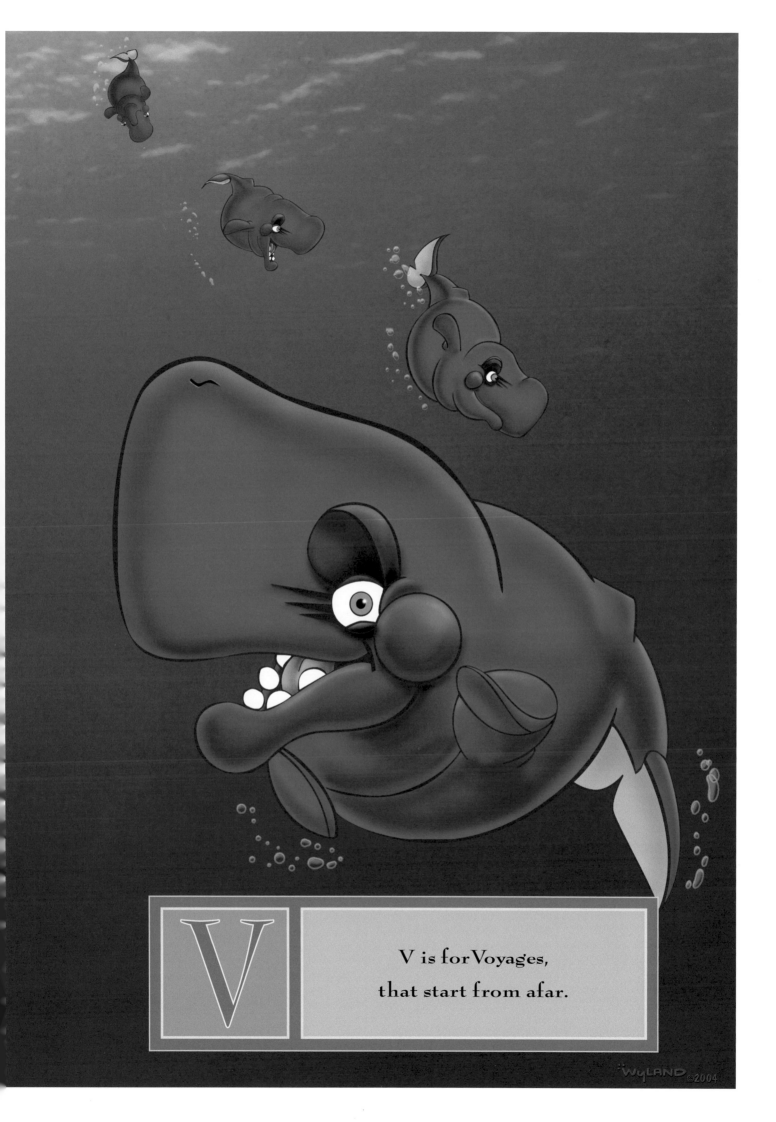

V

V is for Voyages,
that start from afar.

W is for Wild "Bill" fish,
the fastest around.

X marks where a dolphin
named "Ocean" is found.

Y

Y is for Yellow,
the color of "Star."

Z is for Zebra sharks
in a golden sand bar.

So there you have it!
You're just about done,
exploring the A,B, Seas
where learning is fun.

You've seen Spouty's world
where life is in bloom.
Now he's saying goodbye
with a . . .

SHOOSH

And a Zoooooooooom!